WARNING

This book contains sexually explicit scenes and adult language. It may be considered offensive to some readers. This book is for sale to adults ONLY.

* * * * * * * * * * * * * * * * *

Please store your files wisely where they cannot be accessed by underage readers.

DISCLAIMER

ISBN-13: 978-1987863833
ISBN-10: 1987863836

Other Books by Darla Dunbar:

<u>The Romeo Alpha BBW Paranormal Shifter Romance Series</u>

Amanda Walker thinks that she has a normal and boring life. That is until after her 24th birthday. Everything changes when she meets the man who says he was supposed to be her husband. Denying everything the man says, she fights him every step of the way. But after he kidnaps her, Amanda discovers that there are some things about her family that her parents kept a secret all these years. Among the history of the family she learns secrets she thought only happened in story books. Can Amanda tell the difference between truth and lies or is she this mysterious woman that holds the key to a legacy?

<u>Romeo Alpha Blood Lines Romance Series</u>

Twenty-four years have passed in relative peace for Amanda and Romeo. They've raised five children into adulthood and are thoroughly enjoying their lives as the Alpha King and Queen of the werewolves. At twenty-four, Sarina is just stepping into her powers and will be ripe for mating when her birthday comes in two weeks. What no one knows is the danger that lurks just outside their tight knit community. Romeo has made peace with the other clans and has enjoyed that peace, but it will all come crashing down around him when his oldest daughter comes of age to take a mate.

<u>The Alpha Feud BBW Paranormal Shifter Romance Series</u>

Eliza's life consisted of reporting on boring, crowd-pleasing events, like their country livestock fair. With the arrival of two handsome brothers, the lives of Eliza and her best friend, Melissa, are shaken to the core. For Eliza, the arrival of this new man becomes a test of her relationship with her current boyfriend, who she's been happily living with for over six years. Does Hayden, a complete stranger, really wield the power to make Eliza reconsider her relationship with Andrew?

<u>The Alpha Packed BBW Paranormal Shifter Romance Series</u>

Darlene has led a quiet life since suffering through a terrible break-up. She wants nothing more than to spend her time in front of the TV, away from any sort of trouble. But all that goes down the drain when handsome, rugged and rough Idris comes into her life. He is a werewolf on the lookout for his missing pack leader. Darlene quickly finds herself pulled towards this mysterious man and at the same time finds herself falling deeper and deeper into the world of the supernatural.

<u>The Mind Talker Paranormal Romance Series</u>

Ananda finds herself on the run and she's not alone. With help from Jared, a stranger that she just met, the two evade capture by an organization that is intent on hunting her kind. Ananda and Jared are able to read minds. When an unfortunate incident happened involving a disturbed individual that resulted in the death of his schoolmates, the secret organization decided to take action.

<u>The Leather Satchel Paranormal Romance Series</u>

Valtina is stuck in Middle World, unable to pass on to The Afterlife. In order to redeem herself from past deeds done, she must help bring romance back into the world and stop The Dark Side from destroying love in its entirety. Following orders issued by Ladaya and armed with a leather satchel filled with the appropriate tools and weapons, Valtina embraces each mission with enthusiasm.

Get the latest update on new releases from the author at:

https://darladunbar.com/newsletter/

This book is Part Three of "<u>The Daemon Paranormal Romance Chronicles</u>"

Book 1 - The Awakening

Phoebe grew up not knowing her mother. The stranger, Apollo Mikos, claimed to know her mother. After that day, Phoebe's life would change forever.

Book 2 - The Shifter

Phoebe is surprised when her dog, Ace, shows up from nowhere. She is on a mission with Apollo to kill the Qilin. That is the only way that the true leader of daemons will emerge.

Book 3 - Forgotten

Juno has been stirring up trouble that has prolonged the infighting among the daemons. In order to get her to stop, Phoebe agrees to give up a year of her memories. But making deals with a siren is never a good thing. Without her memories, Phoebe's romantic relationship with Supay no longer exists. Instead, she leaves Supay for Apollo.

Book 4 - The Siren's Trap

The unsuspecting couple, Phoebe and Supay, made a deal with Juno to stop the infighting among the daemons. But at what price? An entire year was wiped clean from Phoebe's mind. Now Phoebe was with Apollo. Desperate to get her back, Supay considers Juno's new deal. Is it worth the price to pay for the dubious result? To win back Phoebe's love, Supay will need to be unfaithful to her.

Book 5 - Exposed

Hiding away in Peru, Supay and Phoebe start their own family, away from the chaos and the daemon infighting. Meanwhile, Apollo, heart-broken and lost, is lured into another one of Juno's schemes. Making deals with a siren never turns out right. If Apollo accepts the deal, the love of his life may resent him for the rest of his natural life. If he doesn't take the deal, she is lost to him forever.

Book 6 - The Beginning

As preparations for the war between daemons are underway, everyone must begin to choose. Siding temporarily with Apollo, Juno has a moment to look back on her life and figure out how she arrived at this moment. As she sifts through memories of the past, a specific dark stranger stands out. How far will young Juno go with her new love? More importantly, will her mother, Circe, discover the secret tryst?

Book 7 - The Treachery

Having broken the cardinal rule of the sirens, Juno must take action to save her own life and the life of her unborn child. In order to keep her secret safe from the sisterhood, she must kill her lover and conceal her shame. Will Juno betray the sisterhood and save her lover or will she remain loyal by slaying him instead?

Book 8 - Duplicity

Juno's mother, Circe, discovers her lies and gives her an ultimatum to fix everything. As Juno races against the clock to protect her loved ones from Circe, she makes a final choice that could leave her perpetually unhappy. Left to wander the world alone, Juno realizes that freedom means nothing if there is no one to share it with. The nature of Juno's vendetta—and the means she achieves it with—are finally revealed.

Book 9 - Reconnaissance

As Juno's hunt for the daemon's fortress unfolds, Apollo is left alone wondering if she will truly return to him. Will Juno be able to resist her base instincts? More importantly, will she be able to get to the fortress and return without being spotted? Discover how Juno's stealth mission works out.

Book 10 - The Interrogation

Juno tries to hide her rising fear in the presence of her captors. As her fear mounts, she holds on to the hope that Phoebe or Supay will take pity on her. Before that can happen, she has to come clean to Supay about her past. Could he possibly forgive her for what she has done? Will Juno remain faithful to Apollo or will her siren urges take over? Discover how the confrontation with Supay unfolds.

The Daemon Paranormal Romance Chronicles

Forgotten

Book Three

By Darla Dunbar

Copyright Revelry Publishing 2015

Table of Contents

Chapter One

ROLLING OUT of bed, Phoebe looked on Supay's sleeping form. After spending several weeks with him in Puerto Rico, she decided to move back to Peru, where he lived for most of the year. Her life had taken a strange turn. Instead of working at her fortune telling shop, she was now essentially a kept woman. During the day, they worked together to stop the fighting that kept breaking out in the daemon world. The daemons were essentially a different type of human, and each daemon possessed a unique power. Phoebe could read minds, while Supay could transform into any animal. These unique abilities had given rise to the ancient mythologies of past years. In honor of their ancestors, Phoebe's daemon family had chosen to name all of their children after Greek gods and prophets.

Phoebe threw on a robe and turned on the shower. Over the last few months, she had learned that she was a daemon and that she still had a mother. Her mother, Rhea, had been raped and conceived twin girls. Her twin sister had never made it past birth, but Phoebe had been born. With her gift of mind-reading, she had been in constant pain as an infant because she could see her mother's memories of the rape. Traumatized by the rape and inability to touch her daughter, Rhea had placed Phoebe in foster care. Phoebe finally found out that she was a daemon and about the true story when Apollo came looking for help with killing the Qilin.

Stepping into the shower, Phoebe let the warm water drift along her body. The sensation was pleasant and woke her up. Today, she needed to go with Supay to meet a daemon called Juno. According to the reports, Juno was the daemon behind much of the infighting. With the death of the Qilin, a leader was supposed to appear that would bring peace. According to prophecy, it seemed like Apollo should have been that person. Since he was still brooding over beer about the loss of Phoebe and the killing of the Qilin, Supay had convinced Phoebe that they needed to take action together.

Phoebe heard the shower curtain open. Turning, she saw Supay behind her. Running his hands along her body, he sleepily began to kiss her neck. This harmless gesture was all it took for both of them to become aroused. Since meeting Supay, she had spent the majority of her time dealing with daemons or having sex. Altogether, it was not a bad life.

Pushing him into the shower wall, Phoebe started to run her hands along his cock. The steam from the shower swirled around them. As she touched him, Supay started to wake up and become more responsive. He pushed her against the wall of the shower and lifted her legs around him. Setting her onto his cock, he placed her body against the shower wall. Gradually, he began to thrust quicker and quicker into her. Moaning in pleasure, she orgasmed with him.

As Supay started to wash her body with a loofah, she closed her eyes and enjoyed his touch. Being a daemon had some benefits. According to the other daemons of her tribe, she could never have children with another daemon group. Although this would be terrible when she wanted kids with Supay someday, it meant more enjoyable sex now. Rinsing off, she stepped out of the shower and toweled off.

Before long, Supay and Phoebe were dressed and ready to go. Juno had agreed to meet them in Lima at an Indian restaurant. Together, they got in the car and began the long drive from Cuzco. Finally arriving at the restaurant, Phoebe kissed him. "I love you," she whispered.

He kissed her back. "I love you too." In a moment, their romance would be put aside as they dealt with the daemon world.

Entering the restaurant, they sat down at a table and ordered curry. They had left early to make sure they arrived on time, but it seemed like they may have arrived far too early. After mentioning this, Phoebe was distracted as the most beautiful woman she had ever seen entered the restaurant. The woman had large, dark eyes that were framed by a heart-shaped face. Long black hair hung straight against her body and swayed with her hips when she walked. Although the woman was petite, she managed to have a perfect hourglass figure. Following Phoebe's glance, Supay saw who she was looking at.

Sighing, Supay grimaced. "That would be Juno."
He stood up and waved her over. Ignoring his
outstretched hand, Juno sat down.

"Pleasure to see you again, Supay. Is this the girl
you left me for?" Her musical voice lilted upwards as
she spoke. Phoebe raised an eyebrow and looked at
Supay. He sheepishly shrugged.

"We dated temporarily a few years ago. Juno is just
trying to get under your skin, Phoebe. That's what she
does."

Juno smiled. "How else am I to make life exciting?
Everything is boring, but if you open Pandora's box..."
Her hands fluttered away to show the emotions that left
the box. "Everything can become interesting."

Supay sighed. "That is exactly what we are here for.
We need you to stop causing the fighting. From what I
can tell, you are responsible for most of the trouble."

"Me? You give me far too much credit. I just offer
people alternatives to their current lives by helping to
reach their dreams. If they do something nefarious
along the way, it isn't my fault." She smiled
seductively. Already, Phoebe hated this woman. Her
beautiful body and face hid a vindictive and mean-
spirited personality.

Supay picked up his fork to take a bite of the curry.
After finishing his bite, he looked at Juno again. "If it
isn't your fault, then you would be willing to do
anything to prevent the fighting."

"Why, yes, I suppose that is true. But everything comes at a cost."

Phoebe rolled her eyes. "What is the cost? Do you want money?"

Juno laughed cheerily. "No, of course not. I would never want something as crass as money. Let me think what I would want." She leaned back leisurely and studied the two of them carefully. Phoebe's hand was close to Supay's on the table and it confirmed her suspicions about the relationship. What a happy couple, she thought.

Supay gave up waiting. "Well? What do you want?"

Pausing, Juno seemed to think carefully. "I think that some memories will work fine."

Phoebe frowned. "Memories? What do you mean?"

"If you give me some of your memories, I will stop causing the fighting. You'll still have to stop everyone else involved, but I will step back."

"Whose memories do you want?" Supay frowned. It only took a few weeks of dating Juno for him to realize the spitefulness that she hid in her heart. Anything that she could want or any situation she devised only ended badly. She thrived on creating constant turmoil. In reality, the turmoil is where she drew her power from.

"Her memories," Juno pointed at Phoebe. "Just the memories of the last year or so."

Phoebe was startled. "You want my memories? In trade for peace?"

Laughing again, Juno smiled prettily. "Just for the last year. And I will give your memories back, I just want to borrow them for a few weeks. Maximum of three months, I promise."

Supay looked inquisitively at Juno and then at Phoebe. Without having to consider it, Phoebe nodded. She could give up her memories temporarily if it helped bring peace. Honestly, it seemed such a cheap price. It was such a low cost that it made her suspicious. Supay looked at Juno. "Okay, you can have her memories. First, Phoebe will read your thoughts to see that you are honest in your intentions."

Grasping Juno's hand, Phoebe closed her eyes. The first thought that came up was of Juno and Supay having sex in a meadow. Shocked, Phoebe opened her eyes. Juno just smiled.

"Keep going, dear. I can't help what I was thinking on the top of my mind. If you want the truth, you will have to go deeper."

Grabbing her hand again, Phoebe plunged deeply into her mind. Memories swirled past. In one, Juno stood before a man who was about to kill his brother. Although she did not commit the murder, she urged it on heartlessly. Scene after scene floated past of Juno wreaking disaster and jealousy with just a word or a glance. Scanning through every thought, Phoebe could not see any secondary purposes. When Juno said that she would stick to the peace, she meant it.

Pulling back, she nodded to Supay. Instantaneously, Juno reached forward and touched Phoebe's mind with her own. As each memory from the last year was removed, Phoebe saw it float past.

Sitting in silence, Phoebe did not know where she was. The sensation was a strange one. A beautiful woman sat in front of her and the most attractive man she ever met sat to her right. Not wanting to seem weird, she continued sitting and hoped that she would soon figure out where she was.

Supay looked at her with concern. "Are you okay, Phoebe?" He traced his hand along her cheek in concern. Phoebe drew back from the unexpected touch. Across the table, Juno just smiled.

"Well, Supay, I guess it is my time to leave. Our little damsel in distress here looks like she may need your help." Juno tossed some money on the table casually and walked out.

Turning to Phoebe, Supay tried to hold her hand. She pulled away. "Can you tell me what is going on?" Her voice took on a plaintive note. Without the memories of the last year, she had no clue.

Supay sighed. "That was Juno. She has been causing many of the problems and infighting in the daemon world over the last year. To stop the fighting, you gave her memories from the last year."

"My memories? What's a daemon?"

Grabbing her hand, Supay looked into Phoebe's eyes. "Read my mind. All of the memories that I have of you, you should be able to see."

Cautiously, Phoebe started to look into his mind. The memories that met her were so odd, so unreal that she almost could not believe it. Pulling her hand back shakily, she just sat. "I can't do it."

Concerned, Supay looked at her again. "What do you mean? You should still be able to read my mind."

Phoebe shook her head. "I can't be with you. Not yet. I can see in your memories that I matter greatly, but those aren't my memories. I can't fake feelings that I don't remember myself."

Nodding, Supay stood up. "It will take time. If you want space, I have an old property out of town. You can stay there until you feel like being with me again."

They left the restaurant in silence and started to drive. Stopping at their apartment, Phoebe packed a bag. If his memories were right, she would remember him again in a few months. Until that time, she just wanted to get away from everything.

As dusk fell, they pulled onto an old dirt road. It led to an ancient hut that seemed like it had existed for centuries.

"How long have you had this place?" she asked in an effort to make conversation.

Supay shrugged. "My family has owned it for as long as anyone can remember. It may be a bit dusty on

the inside, but everything should be fine otherwise." He
helped her bring her bags inside and started to kiss her
on the lips. Remembering at the last second that kissing
her would be a bad idea, he ended up pecking her on
the forehead. "Here's my phone number. When you
have your memories, I will be waiting for you." He
looked at her for a moment and she could see the
longing in his glance. She did not say anything and
waited for him to leave.

After he left, she started searching around the hut.
Cleaning supplies were under the sink, so she began to
clean everything. From top to bottom, she scrubbed the
house down in an effort to forget. She did not want to
think about a past she could not remember. If Supay's
memories were true, she may have just let the love of
her life walk away.

Chapter Two

For several days, Phoebe spent her time cleaning. At night, she would read any book she could find in the house until she fell asleep. Early in the morning one day, she woke to the sound of a rooster. Sitting up quickly, she caught sight of it outside of her window. At the same time, a sudden wave of nausea hit her body. Rushing to the bathroom, she threw up. She leaned back against the sink and cursed her luck. Already, she was in such an odd position. Now she had to add the flu to the list of her ailments.

A couple hours passed and Phoebe started to feel a little better. The loneliness of her country life was too much, so she walked into a nearby village and went to a restaurant. An old man waved her in merrily and she ordered a simple dinner. Watching people coming and going, she finished her meal and paid the bill. Stopping at a grocery store, she started to pick out some food. The cabin was quickly becoming understocked. She did not eat a lot, but it had only been filled with canned food when she arrived. Pausing in the shampoo aisle, she selected something that would make her hair softer. As she turned to go to the cashier, her eye caught a pregnancy test. In an instant, she knew—or feared— where her sudden nausea came from.

It was impossible, she thought. From Supay's memories, she had already gathered that she could not have children with any daemon that was not from her family. As a Peruvian, he was definitely not in the same daemon family. Still uncertain, she grabbed two pregnancy tests just in case and checked out.

After paying for her items, Phoebe returned home and took the pregnancy test. It took only several minutes to take, but another five minutes to gather the courage to look at it. A positive result shined brightly from the test strip. Cursing her luck, she took the other test. The same result appeared.

Phoebe went to sit outside. There was no way she could be pregnant. It was impossible; everyone had said that. The only way she could have children was with a daemon or through some outside influence.

Dropping her head into her hands, Phoebe just sat. How could this even happen now? She was pregnant by a man she could not remember and in a different country. Absent-mindedly, she started to finger her jade necklace. Suddenly, she realized what went wrong. The first memory that returned to her now was of the Qilin giving her the necklace. She remembered something! Looking at the necklace, she went into the house and searched through the books. With all of his traveling, Supay had an eclectic mix of language books in the cabin. Pulling a Chinese character book down, she flipped through the pages until she found the character. Fertility. The character on the necklace was an older style, but it clearly meant fertility.

Phoebe sighed. It made sense now. This is why the Qilin told her the necklace was right for her and she would need it someday. The Qilin knew that Phoebe would need it to ever have children with someone else. It would have been better if Phoebe had known that at the time. Closing the book, Phoebe went to shower and get ready for bed. She would figure out what to do in the morning. Although she felt like she ought to say something to Supay, she really did not want to start a relationship again that she could not even remember.

Chapter Three

Waking up early the next morning, Phoebe went for a walk. Birds chirped around her and the sun glowed gently on the blades of grass. Her nausea had subsided sooner this morning. All she had to do was eat some toast after getting out of bed and sip some ginger ale. It was still not particularly pleasurable, but it was bearable.

Wandering into the dusty village, she stopped at the restaurant to have some tea. Sitting at one of the tables was a blonde-haired, attractive man. He looked so familiar, but she could not recall why. While his back was still to her, she realized that she had seen his face in Supay's mind. This was Apollo.

Before she could slip out of the restaurant, Apollo turned around. His face brightened so much that she could not just turn away and leave.

"Phoebe!" He rushed up and gave her a hug. When she did not hug him back, he stepped sheepishly back. "Are you still angry? I missed you so much."

Phoebe shook her head. "No, Juno took my memories temporarily. I don't actually remember you, just what I have been told."

Dismayed, Apollo could not think of what to say. "Well, would you at least join me for breakfast? I'd like a chance to explain my side of everything. Even if you are still angry, we could try being friends again."

Shrugging, Phoebe sat down. "I guess it wouldn't hurt. It would make it easier for me to recall some of my memories."

Smiling again, Apollo sat down opposite her. He ordered a plate of eggs, bacon, and toast for each of them and waited for her to say something.

Phoebe squinted at him. From Supay's memories, she had guessed that she and Apollo were involved previously. She also knew that he was the one who drew her into the hunt for the Qilin. In his own time, he would probably explain more. Supay's memory clearly recalled him saying that he had manipulated her thoughts into liking him and helping him. That would be a difficult betrayal to overcome. It most likely was the reason she left him. She sighed. "How did you even find me? Did Supay tell you?"

"Supay?" Apollo spat the word out distastefully. Supay had done everything he could to hide Phoebe from him. "No, Supay didn't tell me. I ran into Juno and she told me you were here."

"Juno? Oh, Juno." Phoebe didn't even remember the conversation with Juno, but was certainly living with the aftermath. "What did she make you do to get that information?"

"What? Nothing." Apollo frowned. He had been so happy to find Phoebe, he hadn't even thought of that question. Juno was never the type of person to offer help without a cost. "She just told me that you would probably be interested in seeing me and told me where you were."

"Did she tell you about the memories?" Phoebe started to eat the bacon on her plate. The smell of the eggs bothered her.

"No," Apollo said. "What happened?"

"She took my memories of the last year in trade for stepping back from the fight. I only remember what I've been told about you and what I saw in Supay's memory."

Concerned, Apollo reached for her hand. "So you don't actually remember me at all? Why don't you read my mind to see what you're missing?"

Phoebe sighed. "There are two problems with that. The first issue is that I would still only be seeing your thoughts and feelings instead of my own. Second, you are able to manipulate memories. How would I ever be able to trust what I see?"

Apollo shook his head. "I can only suggest thoughts, I can't just lie. Plus, you have my word that I will not manipulate your thoughts. You can see into my mind and I will just let you." He held up his right hand and continued. "Scout's honor."

Biting her lip, Phoebe nodded. Slowly, she reached out and touched his hand. Within an instant, she saw the visit with her mother and the time spent searching for the Qilin. She also felt their first throes of passion and nights in the hotel. As his thoughts drew to a close, she saw the last stand-off with the Qilin.

She looked up. "You loved me? You didn't say it in any of the memories that I just saw."

Apollo nodded, nervously. "Yes, I do. I've been waiting all this time and hoping that you would return. I can't think, eat, or do anything without you. You saw my thoughts. The only reason you left me is because I manipulated your thoughts. But you would have seen sexual fantasies of you anyway if you had looked deep enough into my mind. And I was honestly trying to do the right thing in the hunt for the Qilin. I knew the prophecy probably meant that I wouldn't be the leader. At the same time, I knew that it had to be fulfilled so the real leader could step up in one way or another. If you had just let me explain that day instead of leaving..." He sighed. "That's over now, at any rate."

Phoebe was not sure what to think. From everything in his memory and Supay's mind, it sounded like an honest explanation. She could tell that she had felt hurt and betrayed by him in the past, but she had no recollection of those feelings now. Placing some money on the table for food, she stood up. Apollo looked surprised and waited for her to say something. "If you want, you can come to my cabin and visit for a while. I can't remember the pain, so we may as well start off on better footing."

Standing up, Apollo walked with Phoebe to the cabin. Joking around with her, his blue eyes flashed merrily and Phoebe could see why she had once slept with him. Whenever the path narrowed, she was close enough to his body to smell his aftershave.

Soon, they were back at the cabin. Apollo looked at everything around him. Disappointment welled up as he took the furniture and personal items in. "This is Supay's place."

Phoebe nodded. "I couldn't stay with him after my memories were gone; it just seemed too strange and foreign. He said I could stay here until I figured everything out."

"You were living with him?" Apollo glanced over at her. He had guessed that they might be together, but it sounded like it was more serious than he thought.

"I suppose I was. I don't really remember it now though. Everything just seems so strange. It's like having to learn everything about myself all over again." She flopped down on the couch and flipped through a magazine without thinking about it. Apollo came over to sit next to her.

"You know, if you wanted to leave here, I could help. It's not like you speak Spanish or really know anyone here. I could help you go anywhere or even just return to your fortuneteller shop."

Phoebe smiled. "Thanks, but I'm fine. I still have my own savings. I just figured it was easiest to stay here until I knew of somewhere else that I wanted to go.”

Apollo watched her eyes. As her mood changed, her eyes would shift from hazel to blue to green to gray. It was one of the many things that fascinated him about her. Without thinking, he said the next thought that popped into his head. “May I kiss you?”

Taken aback, Phoebe stopped for a moment and thought about it. “Why not?” It had been weeks since she had last kissed someone. Since she couldn't remember the last year, it wasn't like there was a lot of emotional baggage for her to deal with. Leaning forward, she gently kissed his lips. For months, this was all that Apollo had hoped for and wanted. He put his hand behind her neck and pulled her closer to him. Outside, the birds had finally stopped chirping and crickets had started their song as the evening hours rolled in.

Standing up, Phoebe pulled Apollo with her toward the bedroom. Carefully, he pulled her shirt off and relearned each part of her body. For Phoebe, each touch was a new experience. He caressed the inside of her thighs before unbuttoning her pants. Slipping her pants and underwear off, he kneeled on the ground so that he could kiss her legs. He kissed up the side of her thighs before he spread her legs and put his fingers inside. Gently, he started to play with her clit. The pleasant, teasing sensation brought her to arousal. She pushed his head against her and urged his tongue further inside of her. Unable to bear the longing any more, Phoebe lay down and spread her legs open to accept him. This simple offer was too much to resist. Apollo wanted to draw it out and be gentle, but the sight of her naked and willing was more than he could bear. After months of dreaming about her, he finally entered her body. As she touched his arm, she could read into his mind and see his thoughts. She could feel his desire and see exactly what he was feeling while he was inside her. His desire intermingled with hers in her mind and pushed her to the edge. Screaming out his name, she urged him to go deeper, faster. Their lovemaking took on a frantic pace. Hips rose to meet hips as their two bodies joined as one. Apollo started to reach for a condom, but she pushed him back inside her. Unwilling to wait or ask why, he continued to climax. Throwing his head back, he moaned in rhythm with her as their bodies convulsed together. Within her soul, something broke and she released all of the emotional barriers from before. She was in love.

Lying on the bed, Apollo continued to caress her body. He gently fingered her and felt her wetness mixed with his semen. The thought of orgasming inside her turned him on again. He pulled her on top of him and started to play with her nipples. In response, her nipples quickly hardened. The pregnancy had already made them more sensitive and his fingers had tapped into this heightened pleasure. As his cock hardened again, she moaned. After so long without sex, she would not be able to refuse another round. She wanted him. With every fiber of her being, she wanted him inside her again. Straddling his body, she brought him into her. Unlike other days, she would not be able to tease or toy with him. She wanted to orgasm again and nothing would stop her. Rocking her hips violently against his,

she felt herself orgasm. It wasn't enough. Until all of
the desire in her body was spent, she would not and did
not want to stop. Her hips rose and fell in rhythm as she
gained enough control of her senses to tease him.
Staying around his head, she managed to titillate and
taunt his cock. Unable to take it any longer, he forced
himself into her body. He rolled over and forced her
beneath him. Holding her wrists together, Apollo
stopped her from moving away. He thrust again and
again. Each thrust penetrated deeper into her body. As
her body started to convulse into another orgasm, the
clenching of her muscles drew him deep inside of her.
He came again in a fit of ecstasy.

Exhausted and spent, the pair fell asleep in each
other's arms. Before they fell asleep completely,
Phoebe turned to Apollo.

"Do you really believe we were fated to be
together?" she said sleepily.

He nodded. "I love you."

"I love you too."

The next morning, Apollo was waiting at the table
for her with a cup of coffee. He offered her a cup, but
she turned it down. He asked her to sit. "So Phoebe,
what do you want to do? If you want to come away
with me, I would love that. I will take you anywhere in
the world. If you do not want to stay with me when
your memories return, I understand. I just can't take the

risk of losing you again without at least trying to convince you to be with me."

Phoebe sat down at the table. She had no idea where she wanted to go or what she wanted to do. Already, they had spent a day together and she had managed not to tell him that she was pregnant. How was she going to tell him that after they traveled? At the same time, she could not just stay here forever. Supay would expect her to decide or return to ask her to be with him. Although she missed her old home, she was not that girl anymore. Even if she did not remember the last year, she knew that she just could not go back and pick up her former life.

She nodded to Apollo. "I can't guarantee that I will want to be with you when my memories return. All I know is that I don't want to stay here. If you are okay with the possibility that I may end up leaving, I will come with you."

Ecstatic, Apollo jumped up from his seat and gave her a kiss. "That's perfect. Pack your bags and we will book the next flight to Europe. I only have a few weeks to show you my love before you need to decide whether to be with me or not. I'll get the car."

Apollo left the cabin and Phoebe looked around the room pensively. She packed her bags quickly and tried not to think about the big decision she had just made. As she turned off the lights, she saw Supay's number tacked to the wall. She hesitated and then grabbed the piece of paper. Although she could not bring herself to call him now, she would have to at least let him know at some point that she was gone. Flipping off the switch, she said goodbye to the past.

-To be continued in Book 4-

If you enjoyed this title, I would appreciate your leaving a review of the book. Good reviews encourage an author to write as well as help books to sell. Good reviews can be just a few short sentences describing what you liked about the book without having a spoiler. If you could spend 30 seconds writing a review, I would appreciate it: you can review this title right now at your favorite retailer.

Here is a preview of the **next story** you may enjoy:

The Siren's Trap - The Daemon Paranormal Romance Chronicles, Book 4

PHOEBE STARED out at the ocean. In La Coruna, or A Coruna as the locals called it, the ocean was everything. Next to her was the world's oldest lighthouse. It was said to have been built by Hercules himself in ancient times. After several weeks of being in Spain and an excellent grammar book, she was finally starting to pick up on the language. Right now was not the time for studying. This moment was hers alone to stare into the great expanse of ocean before her. Across those waters, she had helped to search for a new leader, find the Qilin, and fell in love.

Already, memories were starting to float back into her mind. The spiteful witch, Juno, had taken her memories temporarily. As memories of Supay started to flow back, Phoebe realized why. Juno was not intent on leading daemons to take over the world or even gain power. They had overestimated her goals. From everything that Phoebe could figure out, Juno just wanted to cause trouble. She thrived on causing hurt to people. Although Juno had agreed to stay out of the infighting, she had managed to split Supay and Phoebe apart. Now, Phoebe was across the world with Apollo. He had rented a condo near the beach and spent each day trying to prove his love. At first, his attempts had been endearing. Now, it felt like he was smothering her. In reality, nothing may have been different. She had just started to change as her memories came back. Phoebe remembered Supay's cute quirks and his dedication to always doing what was right. She also remembered her own disapproval of Apollo and his intention to kill the Qilin. Alone at the edge of the world, there was no escape from her memories.

Picking her way down the rocks, Phoebe got as close to the ocean as possible. The few tourists that were there spoke Spanish, since La Coruna was a Spanish-tourist destination. On occasion, she ran into the random English family who had decided to take holiday there. The number of English speakers that she had met could be counted on one hand. It made for a lonely existence, but she felt less alone as her Spanish improved. The warmth of Spain and the salty sea air were a welcome change from the thin air at Cuzco.

Sitting down on a rock, Phoebe started to cry. Since finding out she was pregnant, her hormones had gone haywire. It did not help that she truly was in a bad situation. She was stuck in Spain with Apollo and could not bring herself to tell him that she was pregnant. Since she was only a few months along, it still was not noticeable. Even worse, she could not bring herself to call Supay and tell him that she was going to have their child. Unless Supay stopped by the cabin, he may not even know that she was gone. Even worse, he may have already realized she was gone. If so, he would be frantic with worry.

If you enjoyed this sample then look for **The Siren's Trap - The Daemon Paranormal Romance Chronicles, Book 4**.

Here is a preview of **another story** you may enjoy:

TYPICALLY, on a normal day, Ananda woke up securely warm and cocooned in the down-filled blankets of her bed. The window over her bed had no blinds, only sheer curtains that fully allowed the rising sun to shine brightly, illuminating the room and waking her gradually. What she did not normally wake up to is her skin overwrought with sensitive nerves, itchiness demanding her attention, and skin feeling one degree away from boiling. Slitting her eyes open, Ananda could see moonlight seeping through a crack in curtains that absolutely did not belong to her, creating random shadow patterns on the wall that did nothing to calm the frantic beating of her heart. If not for the familiar arm stretched out around her waist, she would have jerked out of bed. As it was she simply gazed around while letting her mind catch up to the situation.

Shifting slightly, Ananda was unpleasantly surprised when a bolt of pain shot down her spine. "Ow ow, fuck ow! What the hell did you do to me?!"

"…Nothing that you didn't ask for."

The unexpected answer pushed a small huff of laughter between Ananda's lips until her breath was coming out in wheezing gasps. She could feel herself beginning to panic and who could blame her? Her skin felt like it was on fire, she was in bed with a man she met barely a day ago and she was running from some unknown entity that broke into the house she shared with a best friend who she was afraid she'd either never see again or would only hear about on the news. All things considered, panicking was the tamest thing she could be doing at this point when compared to the alternatives such as running screaming into oncoming traffic.

Ananda considered calling her parents and then quickly pushed that thought from her mind. All she needed was for them to once again think that she was crazy when she explained about hearing other people's voices and apparently finding someone who shared that same gift. Not to mention having to explain to them that she was currently shacked up with said person in a slightly sleazy hotel room after having explosive sex that left her catatonic for…

"How long have I been out?" Ananda would have been surprised by the breathy quality of her voice if she weren't still trying to gain control of her body and regulate her breathing. The hand that had been resting on her stomach was now moving softly in a circle that, amazingly, was helping her regain her sense of calm. That musky, citrusy scent was back and curling softly about her, somehow cooling the heat that settled right underneath her skin. She could feel the aches from their previous bedroom activities diminishing until all she felt was a dull buzz. "God that's like catnip or something…" Her voice trailed off into a satisfied gasp. The hand on her stomach paused for a moment but once again continued after she whimpered softly.

If you enjoyed this sample then look for **Heat - The Mind Talker Paranormal Romance Series, Book 3.**

Other Books by Darla Dunbar

- The Romeo Alpha BBW Paranormal Shifter Romance Series

- Romeo Alpha Blood Lines Romance

- The Alpha Feud BBW Paranormal Shifter Romance Series

- The Alpha Packed BBW Paranormal Shifter Romance Series

- The Mind Talker Paranormal Romance Series

- The Leather Satchel Paranormal Romance Series

Get the latest update on new releases from the author at:

https://darladunbar.com/newsletter/

About the Author - Darla Dunbar

Darla has been interested in paranormal romance since she was a teenager in high school. It was then that she discovered she could fulfill her fantasies through her writing.

Observing people and human behavior in the area of romance has always been one of her favorite pastimes. Combining that with an overactive imagination is a sure fire way of coming up with interesting themes.

Connect with Darla Dunbar

I really appreciate you reading my book! Here are my social media coordinates:

Friend me on Facebook: https://www.facebook.com/darladunbar/

Follow me on Twitter: https://twitter.com/DarlDunbar

Check me out on Goodreads: https://www.goodreads.com/author/show/8425857.Darla_Dunbar

Subscribe to my newsletter: https://darladunbar.com/newsletter/

Visit my website: https://darladunbar.com/